characters cr... ...ild

lau... ...ild

But
excuse me
THAT is my
book

PUFFIN

Charlie and Lola ®

Text based on script written by Bridget Hurst and Carol Noble

Illustrations from the TV animation produced by Tiger Aspect

With special thanks to Leigh Hodgkinson

PUFFIN BOOKS

UK | USA | Canada | Ireland | Australia
India | New Zealand | South Africa

Puffin Books is part of the Penguin Random House group of companies
whose addresses can be found at global.penguinrandomhouse.com.

puffinbooks.com

First published in hardback 2005
This edition published in paperback 2006
Reissued 2016
012

Printed and bound in China

A CIP catalogue record for this book is available from the British Library

ISBN: 978-0-141-50053-9

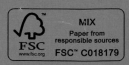

MIX
Paper from
responsible sources
FSC™ C018179

I have this little sister Lola.
She is small and very funny.
Lola loves reading and she really loves books.
But at the moment there is
one book that is extra specially special.

One day, Lola said,
    "Charlie, Dad says he will take
us to the library and we must go
    right now and get
        Beetles, Bugs and Butterflies."

Lola loves Beetles, Bugs and Butterflies.

I say,
    "But Dad took that book out
                for you last time...
And the time before that..."

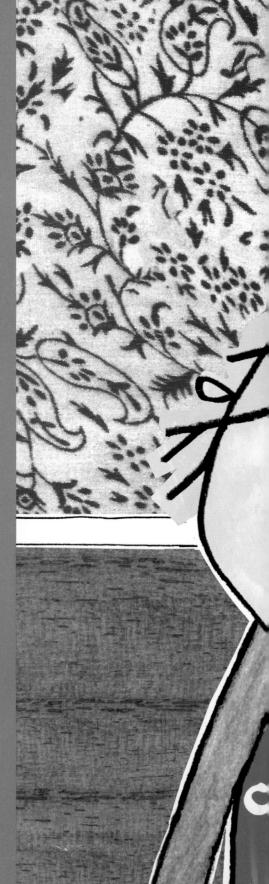

Then Lola says,
     "But Charlie, Beetles, Bugs and
Butterflies is a very special book
that is my favourite
and I really
need it.

Now.

     Now.

          Now.

               Now.

                    Now!

Don't you know
Beetles, Bugs and Butterflies
is the best book in the whole world?"

And Lola says,

"You see, Charlie,

the bugs are quite buggy

and the butterflies are really beautiful and

the beetles are...

very silly.

The beetle gets stuck!
And his legs are very funny!

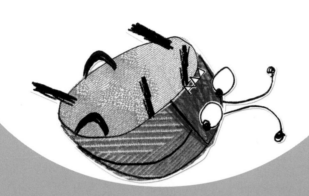

And he

can't

get

down!"

I say,
"I know that, Lola.
Come on.
Dad's waiting."

"All his funny
little legs. Charlie!"

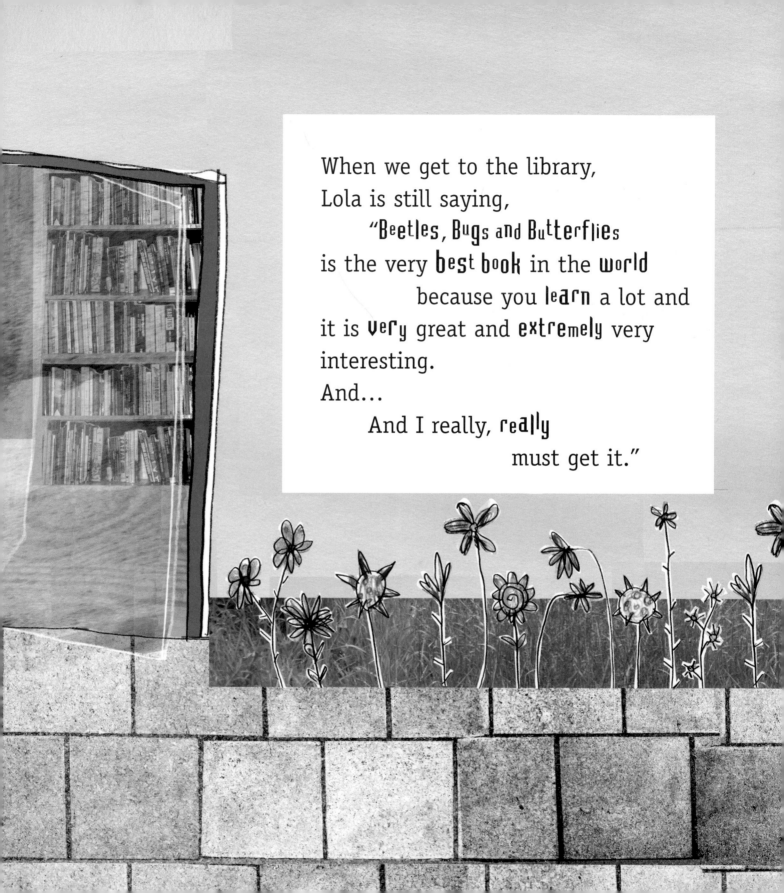

When we get to the library,
Lola is still saying,
        "Beetles, Bugs and Butterflies
is the very best book in the world
                because you learn a lot and
it is very great and extremely very
interesting.
And...
        And I really, really
                        must get it."

When we get inside
　　　I have to say,

"Shh! Lola, it's a library.
　　　We have to be quiet."

Lola says,
"But I can't find
　　　my book, Charlie."

And I say,
　　　"Then why don't you
try looking for it

with all the books
　　　beginning with B?"

So Lola says,
"B, B, B... Where is **my** book?
Where can it be?"
I say, "Lola! Be quiet!"
She says,
"I am being quiet, Charlie!"
I say, "Shhhhh!"

She says, "I am **shushing!**
It's not there!
My book's not there!"

I say, "Lola! Be quiet!"
Lola says, "But Charlie, my book is lost!
It is completely not there!"

I say,
"Lola, remember this is a library
        so someone must have borrowed it."

Lola says,
        "But Beetles, Bugs
                and Butterflies
        is my book."

I say,
"But it's not your library.
        Someone else obviously
wanted to read your book."

Lola says,
"But they can't. It's my book."

So I say, "Lola, just think.
There are hundreds and hundreds of other books
in the library to choose from.

There are spy books and dinosaur books. Adventure books

and scary books.

Books about princes,
    aeroplanes and astronauts.

Books about castles,
    dragons and volcanoes,

monsters,

mountains and pixies.   And books about Romans."

Romersk

فورح

România

I say,

"Look! **Romans!** This one tells you
    all about **history** in the **Roman** times.
Like how the **Romans** built long, straight roads
    and rode chariots and had
fights with swords."

oma li

rumi

римский

ro-man

római

римски

로마

But Lola says,
"Too many
big
words,
Charlie.

Römer

zymski

Rómv

latinluk

România

"My **book** has got **pictures** that I really like."

So I say,
"OK, Lola, let's try to find
a book with more pictures and less words.

How about this? An encyclopedia?
It's got millions of drawings and millions of facts.
You can learn about **everything**.
Look, this page is all about helicopters."

"It's too loud, Charlie! I don't really like encyclo... ped... these **big** books.

You see, Charlie, I am **very** right,
Beetles, Bugs and Butterflies
is the **best** book ever."

I say,
"You might be right, Lola,
        but see what you
    think of this...
        It's a pop-up book."

But Lola says,
    "A book that has

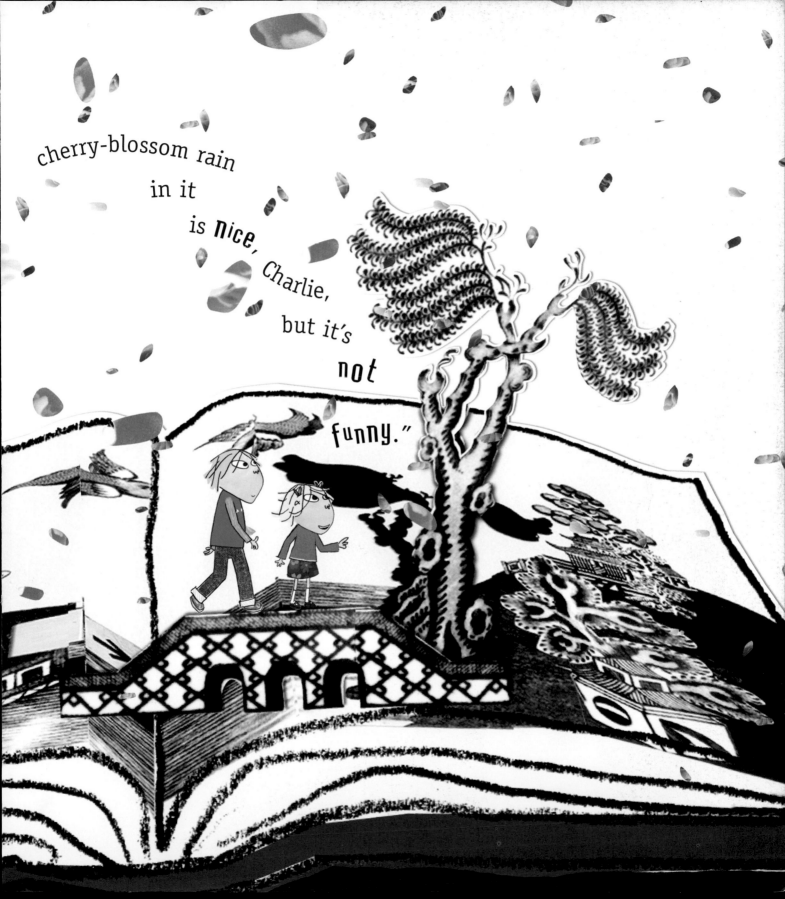

Then Lola says,
"Beetles, Bugs and Butterflies
is really funny
and makes me

laugh

and

laugh

and

laugh..."

I say,
"So it's an **animal** book you want.
A book with... lots of pictures... a story...
no **big** words... and animals that make you laugh."
Lola says, "Yep."
I say, "How about **this**, Lola?! Cheetahs and Chimpanzees."
Lola says, "Are there
beetles, bugs and butterflies in it?!"
I say, "No, there are
cheetahs and chimpanzees.
Give it a try, Lola. Please."

Lola says, "OK, Charlie,
I will. But it won't
be as good as...

Beetles,
Bugs
and
Butterflies!

Oh no, Charlie! Look!
That girl's got My book!
I don't think she knows
it is
My book!

No, noO...

Just wait...

That's **my**...

That's **my**...

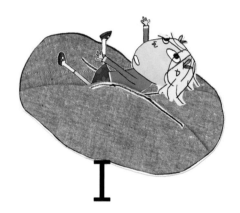

I

just

like

My book,

Charlie!"

Lola says,
"I want **My book**, Charlie!"
And I say,
"But you said you would try
Cheetahs and Chimpanzees."

Lola says,
"Well... I'll try it
but it won't be as good
as Beetles, Bugs and Butterflies."

But then Lola says,
"Oh! Look at that. The cheetahs are very fast and the chimpanzees

are very cheeky and in fact, you know what, Charlie...?

This **book** is probably
        the **most best book** in the whole wide world
    because it is so **interesting** and so **lovely**
and you know it has the **absolutely** best **pictures** of **any book ever**
        and the baby **chimps** are very **funny**..."